THE BABY-SITTERS CLUB®

DAWN AND THE IMPOSSIBLE THREE

DON'T MISS THE OTHER
BABY-SITTERS CLUB GRAPHIC NOVELS!

KRISTY'S GREAT IDEA

THE TRUTH ABOUT STACEY

MARY ANNE SAVES THE DAY

CLAUDIA AND MEAN JANINE

KRISTY'S BIG DAY

ANN M. MARTIN

THE BABY-SITTERS CLUB®

DAWN AND THE IMPOSSIBLE THREE

A GRAPHIC NOVEL BY

GALE GALLIGAN

WITH COLOR BY BRADEN LAMB

Library of Congress Control Number: 2016960080

ISBN 978-1-338-06730-9 (hardcover)
ISBN 978-1-338-88827-0 (paperback)

10 9 8 7 6 5 4 3 2 1 23 24 25 26 27

Printed in China 62
This edition first printing, April 2023

Edited by Cassandra Pelham Fulton and David Levithan
Book design by Phil Falco
Creative Director: David Saylor

For Aunt Dot

A. M. M.

Eternal thanks to Mom, Dad, Lori, A. M. M.,
Raina Telgemeier, Cassandra Pelham, David Saylor,
David Levithan, Phil Falco, Sheila Marie Everett, Braden Lamb,
John Green, Dave Roman, Rachel Young, Ngozi Ukazu,
Dave Valeza, and all my beloved friends,
family, and grads.

And to Patrick, who gets his very own line
because he is my favorite boy.

G. G.

KRISTY THOMAS
PRESIDENT

CLAUDIA KISHI
VICE PRESIDENT

DAWN SCHAFER
ALTERNATE OFFICER

MARY ANNE SPIER
SECRETARY

STACEY MCGILL
TREASURER

CHAPTER 1
I'M STILL NOT SURE WHAT THE BIG DEAL ABOUT NEW ENGLAND WINTERS IS.
TKTKTK
I'VE ONLY LIVED HERE A FEW MONTHS.
LAST FALL MY PARENTS SPLIT UP, AND MOM DECIDED TO UPROOT US FROM SUNNY CALIFORNIA...
huff puff
TKTKTK
TO FREEZING CONNECTICUT.
dinga ling
I'LL GET IT! I'LL GET IT!
HI, CLAIRE!
MY NAME IS DAWN SCHAFER, AND I'M THE NEWEST MEMBER OF THE BABY-SITTERS CLUB.
OR, WELL, I WAS.

I'm DAWN. REMEMBER ME?
nod
CAN I COME IN?
...
OH, IT'S YOU, DAWN. **TERRIFIC!**
YOU'RE RIGHT ON TIME.
nod
IF YOU NEED ME, JUST CALL THE LIBRARY AND TELL THEM I'm IN THE TRUSTEES MEETING, OKAY? THE NUMBER IS BY THE PHONE.
AND THE EMERGENCY NUMBERS ARE IN THEIR USUAL SPOT.
shff
GOT IT!
MALLORY'S UPSTAIRS DOING HER HOMEWORK, BUT SHE'LL BE DOWN SOON.
MARGO'S IN THE REC ROOM, AND NICKY'S AT THE BARRETTS' PLAYING WITH BUDDY.
I WAS BABY-SITTING FOUR OF THE EIGHT PIKE CHILDREN THAT AFTERNOON.
OKAY.
THOSE TWO GO BACK AND FORTH ALL THE TIME, SO YOU'LL PROBABLY SEE THEM LATER.

BE GOOD FOR DAWN, PUMPKIN.
WEAR YOUR JACKET IF YOU GO OUT, IT'S CHILLY TODAY.
kiss
SHE WOULDN'T HAVE TO TELL **ME** TWICE.
LET'S GO SEE WHAT MARGO IS DOING, OKAY?
nod
...RIIIGHT BY THE SEAAAA
AND SPLASHED IN THE SPARKLY WAVES
IN A LAND CALLED HAMMY LEEEEEE
BRAVO!
BRAVO!!
clapclapclap
DAWN!

WHAT'S EIGHT TIMES SEVEN?
HI, MAL. YOU KNOW THAT ONE.

THIS IS MALLORY.
...
FIFTY-SIX?

SHE'S HELPED US BABY-SIT BEFORE.
RIGHT!
THANKS! THAT'S ALL I HAD LEFT.

SNACK TIME??
SURE.

whoosh
IN FACT, TODAY WILL BE HER FIRST DAY AS AN OFFICIAL JUNIOR MEMBER OF THE BSC.

SO, DAWN, HOW'S YOUR NEW-OLD HOUSE?
OH, IT'S FINE.
NEW-OLD. IT SOUNDS FUNNY, BUT IT'S KIND OF TRUE.
OUR NEW HOUSE WAS BUILT WAY BACK IN 1795!
AND HOW'S YOUR MOOOOOM?
WEEEEEELL...

SHE'S STILL GOING OUT ON INTERVIEWS...
LOOKING FOR A JOB...
COME ON, DAWN!
AND SHE'S STILL GOING OUT WITH MR. SPIER.
YESSSSS!
WHEN MOM, MY BROTHER, JEFF, AND I MOVED TO CONNECTICUT, I BECAME CLOSE FRIENDS WITH MARY ANNE SPIER.
MARY ANNE AND I DID A LITTLE DIGGING AND FOUND OUT THAT OUR PARENTS USED TO DATE!
Dearest Richie,
THEY'VE BEEN THROUGH A LOT SINCE THEN -- MY MOM IS DIVORCED, AND MARY ANNE'S DAD IS WIDOWED.
WE REINTRODUCED THEM, AND IT SEEMS TO BE GOING REALLY WELL!
thud
AUUUUUUUGH!!
WHAT WAS THAT?

SUZI!
IT'S SUZI BARRETT.
AND THIS IS HER BROTHER, BUDDY.
SHE FELL COMING UP THE STEPS. I THINK SHE SKINNED HER KNEE.
OWWWW.
I'M DAWN, SUZI.
WHY DON'T YOU COME IN AND WE'LL WASH YOUR CUT AND FIND YOU A BANDAGE?
WE HAVE BAND-AIDS WITH DINOSAURS ON THEM.
THANKS.

hydrogen Peroxide
8 FL OZ
glug
AT LEAST IT'S NOT AS BAD AS NICKY'S FINGER.
WHAT'S THAT?
A FEW MONTHS AGO, I WAS BABY-SITTING THE BOYS AND THEY WERE PLAYING VOLLEYBALL.
NICKY LOOKED AWAY FOR A MOMENT AND...
BAM! THE BALL SLAMMED INTO HIS FINGER.
IT WAS IN A CAST FOR MONTHS.
I TOOK CARE OF ALL THE KIDS WHILE MOM AND DAD DROVE NICKY TO THE EMERGENCY ROOM.
THIS HAPPENED WHEN YOU WERE IN CHARGE OF HIM?
I MEAN, IT WAS AN ACCIDENT.

SUZI AND BUDDY STAYED OVER FOR THE REST OF THE DAY.
WE WATCHED SESAME STREET...
MADE A DINOSAUR VILLAGE...
AND THEN IT WAS TIME TO PICK UP MARY ANNE FOR OUR BABY-SITTERS CLUB MEETING.
GO ON WITHOUT ME. I'LL HEAD OVER IN A FEW MINUTES.
OKAY, SEE YOU THERE.

BUT I COULDN'T STOP THINKING ABOUT THE STORY MALLORY TOLD ME.
WAS SHE REALLY READY TO BE A FULL-FLEDGED BABY-SITTER?
I'D HAVE TO TALK TO THE GIRLS ABOUT IT.
HEY, GUESS WHAT?!
GREAT NEWS!

CHAPTER 2

WHAT? WHAT IS IT?
DAD JUST CALLED.
HE SAID NOT TO EXPECT HIM FOR DINNER TONIGHT.
SO?
HE SAID NOT TO EXPECT HIM...
BECAUSE HE'S TAKING YOUR MOM OUT!
twirl
OH! ANOTHER DATE!!
DAD **NEVER** USED TO DO SPUR-OF-THE-MOMENT THINGS.
BUT HE SAID HE GOT THE IDEA ABOUT FIVE MINUTES AGO!
I CAN'T BELIEVE IT.

I KNEW ONE REASON MARY ANNE WAS SO HAPPY ABOUT OUR PARENTS DATING.
IT WAS BECAUSE MY MOTHER TOOK MR. SPIER'S MIND OFF MARY ANNE.
Sighhh
HE USED TO MAKE SO MANY RULES FOR HER.
ABOUT HER HAIR, HER CLOTHES, HER CURFEW...
IT WAS AMAZING THAT SHE COULD REMEMBER THEM ALL.
BUT NOW MARY ANNE CAN WEAR CONTACTS IF SHE WANTS, SHE CAN SPEND HER BABY-SITTING MONEY IF SHE SAVES HER ALLOWANCE, AND SHE CAN BUY HER OWN CLOTHES!
YOU KNOW WHAT I'M GOING TO START DOING?
REDECORATING MY ROOM.
NO! REALLY??
IT'S SO COOL SEEING HOW SHE EXPRESSES HERSELF.

I USED TO THINK THAT THE ONLY WAY I'D BE ABLE TO REDECORATE WAS IF MY FATHER LOST HIS MIND.
I GUESS HE DID LOSE IT -- OVER YOUR MOTHER.
THANKS A LOT!
OH, YOU KNOW WHAT I MEAN. I THINK IT'S GREAT.
GREAT THAT THEY'RE GOING OUT, OR GREAT THAT HE'S LOST HIS MIND?
BOTH.
WHAT ARE YOU GOING TO DO TO YOUR ROOM?
I'M GOING TO TAKE ALL THE KID STUFF OFF MY WALLS AND PUT UP POSTERS AND PHOTOGRAPHS.
THAT'S ALL I CAN AFFORD TO DO.
BUT IF I CAN GET MY DAD TO AGREE, I'D LOVE A NEW BEDSPREAD, RUG, CURTAINS, AND WALLPAPER.
EVERYTHING IN MY ROOM IS PINK, AND I CAN'T **STAND** PINK!
ding dong

OH, DAWN AND MARY ANNE. HELLO.
CLAUDIA IS UPSTAIRS AWAITING YOUR ARRIVAL.
HI, JANINE.
THIS IS JANINE, CLAUDIA'S SISTER.
SHE'S ALREADY TAKING COLLEGE-LEVEL CLASSES, EVEN THOUGH SHE'S ONLY IN HIGH SCHOOL.
HOW'S MIMI TODAY?
OH! SHE IS DOING VERY WELL.
WE WERE JUST WORKING ON HER FLASH CARDS TOGETHER.
IS THAT MY MARY ANNE?
MIMI IS CLAUDIA'S GRANDMOTHER. WE WERE ALL REALLY WORRIED WHEN SHE HAD A STROKE A FEW MONTHS AGO -- ESPECIALLY MARY ANNE.
MIMI!
THEY'VE ALWAYS HAD A SPECIAL RELATIONSHIP.

I HEAR YOU'RE WORKING ON FLASH CARDS RIGHT NOW.
YES. MANY, MANY FLASH CARDS.
SHE STILL MIXES IN JAPANESE WORDS SOMETIMES, BUT I REALLY DO THINK THEY'RE HELPING.
OH, IT'S 5:30. YOUR CLUB WILL BE EXPECTING YOU.
THANKS, JANINE!

I KNOW... I LEFT SOME...
RIGHT AROUND HERE...
THIS IS CLAUDIA, OUR VICE PRESIDENT.
YES!
gummi
STACEY'S OUR TREASURER. SHE MOVED HERE FROM NEW YORK CITY A LITTLE WHILE BEFORE I CAME.
WE'RE UP TO FOURTEEN DOLLARS.
NOT BAD.
MAYBE WE SHOULD GET MORE STUFF FOR THE KID-KITS?
KRISTY IS THE CLUB'S FOUNDER AND PRESIDENT.
SHE DIDN'T LIKE ME MUCH AT FIRST, BUT I THINK WE'RE ALL RIGHT NOW.
AM I LATE?

HEY, MALLORY! YOU CAN SIT WHEREVER.
WANT SOME?
UM...
THANKS.
AHEM.
MALLORY, WE WANTED YOU TO COME TO TODAY'S MEETING FOR TWO REASONS.
FIRST, SO YOU CAN SEE HOW OUR CLUB RUNS, AND SECOND, SO WE CAN DECIDE, IF, UM...
UM...
SO WE CAN GET AN IDEA OF HOW WELL...HMM.
HOW MUCH EXPERIENCE YOU'VE HAD.
RIGHT. AND TO FIND OUT HOW YOU HANDLE CERTAIN SITUATIONS.
WELL, I'VE BEEN TAKING CARE OF MY BROTHERS AND SISTERS FOR YEARS.
I KNOW HOW TO CHANGE DIAPERS AND FIX FORMULAS. I'VE ALWAYS --
MALLORY, WOULD YOU MIND TELLING US ABOUT NICKY'S FINGER?

THAT ACCIDENT SHOULDN'T HAVE HAPPENED.
YOU SHOULD HAVE BEEN WATCHING HIM.
BUT I --
WE HAVE TO BE REALLY CAREFUL ABOUT WHO WE ACCEPT INTO THE CLUB.
WE'VE HAD SOME TROUBLE IN THE PAST WITH SITTERS WHO WERE... UNRELIABLE.
BUT I **AM** RELIABLE.
AND I **WAS** WATCHING NICKY.
A-AND I KNOW **EVERYTHING** ABOUT TAKING CARE OF KIDS.
THEN YOU WON'T MIND TAKING A **TEST.**

ALL RIGHT. QUESTION ONE.
DURING THAT MEETING, WE ALTERNATED BETWEEN TAKING CLUB CALLS...
ringgg
I'LL GET IT!
AND GRILLING MALLORY.
AT WHAT AGE DOES A BABY CUT HIS FIRST TOOTH?
EIGHT MONTHS.
WRONG. MARY ANNE, KEEP SCORE.
WHAT? BUT MY SISTER --
SECOND QUESTION. WHAT TEETH DOES THE BABY USUALLY CUT FIRST?
DO YOU WANT THE BREWERS NEXT THURSDAY?
UM... THE MIDDLE ONES ON THE BOTTOM?
ARE YOU ASKING US OR TELLING US?
TELLING... YOU?
AHEM.
DESCRIBE THE STRUCTURE OF THE DIVESTIVE SYSTEM.
THAT'S DIGESTIVE.

AGHHHHH! THIS IS RIDICULOUS!
YOU CAN'T HONESTLY TELL ME THAT YOU ALL KNOW THE ANSWERS TO ALL OF THESE QUESTIONS.
MALLORY, THIS IS IMPORTANT BABY-SITTING KNOWLEDGE.
WELL, THEN, GIVE ME A CHANCE TO SHOW YOU WHAT I DO KN--
ring ring
HELLO, BABY-SITTERS CLUB.
NEXT THURSDAY AFTERNOON?
HOW MANY?
BUDDY AND SUZI! IS THIS MRS. BARRETT?
DAWN, YOU'RE THE ONLY ONE FREE ON THURSDAY.
I LOOK FORWARD TO SEEING YOU THEN.
I'M BABY-SITTING FOR THE BARRETTS!
YOU HAVEN'T EVEN GIVEN ME A CHANCE!
WE'VE GOT TO BE CAREFUL ABOUT THESE THINGS, MALLORY.
KRISTY...
WHY DON'T WE HAVE A TRIAL RUN?

MALLORY GOES ON A JOB WITH ONE OF US.
IT CAN BE FOR THE PIKES, EVEN.
THAT SOUNDS FAIR.
OKAY, MALLORY?
ALL RIGHT.
IT LOOKS LIKE RIGHT NOW, OUR NEXT APPOINTMENT WITH YOUR FAMILY IS...NEXT SATURDAY. DOES THAT WORK FOR YOU?
THAT'S FINE.
THEN I HEREBY DISMISS TODAY'S MEETING OF THE BABY-SITTERS CLUB.

Divestive system
esophagus
stomach
large intestine
small intestine
apendix

CHAPTER 3
I GOT BACK HOME THAT EVENING JUST AS MOM WAS ON HER WAY OUT TO MEET MR. SPIER FOR DINNER.
I'M HOME!
HONEY, I'M LEAVING!
I SHOULD BE BACK IN A FEW HOURS.
OKAY, HAVE FUN.
DINNER'S READY FOR YOU AND JEFF.
OKAY.
IT'S SITTING IN THE POT ON THE STOVE.
OKAY --
AND THERE'S SALAD IN THE FRIDGE.
OKAAAY.
click
MOM, COME BACK HERE.
WHAT?

ONLY ONE EARRING
RUBBER BAND
PRICE TAG

MOM, FOR HEAVEN'S SAKE.
WHAT WOULD I DO WITHOUT YOU, DAWN?
snap

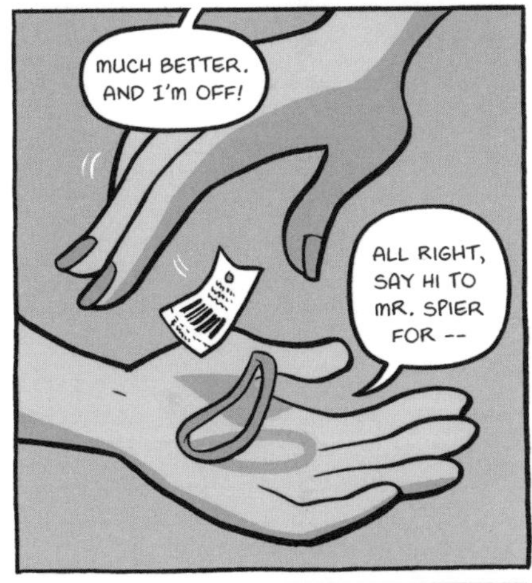
MUCH BETTER. AND I'M OFF!
ALL RIGHT, SAY HI TO MR. SPIER FOR --

. . .

EARRING!

UUUUGH.
glorp
LEFTOVER STEW.

C'MON, C'MON.

PIZZA

HEY, JEFF!
ORGANIC FROZEN PIZZA?
YES, **PLEASE.**

ding!

ring
rin

ring ring ring
BOOOOO.

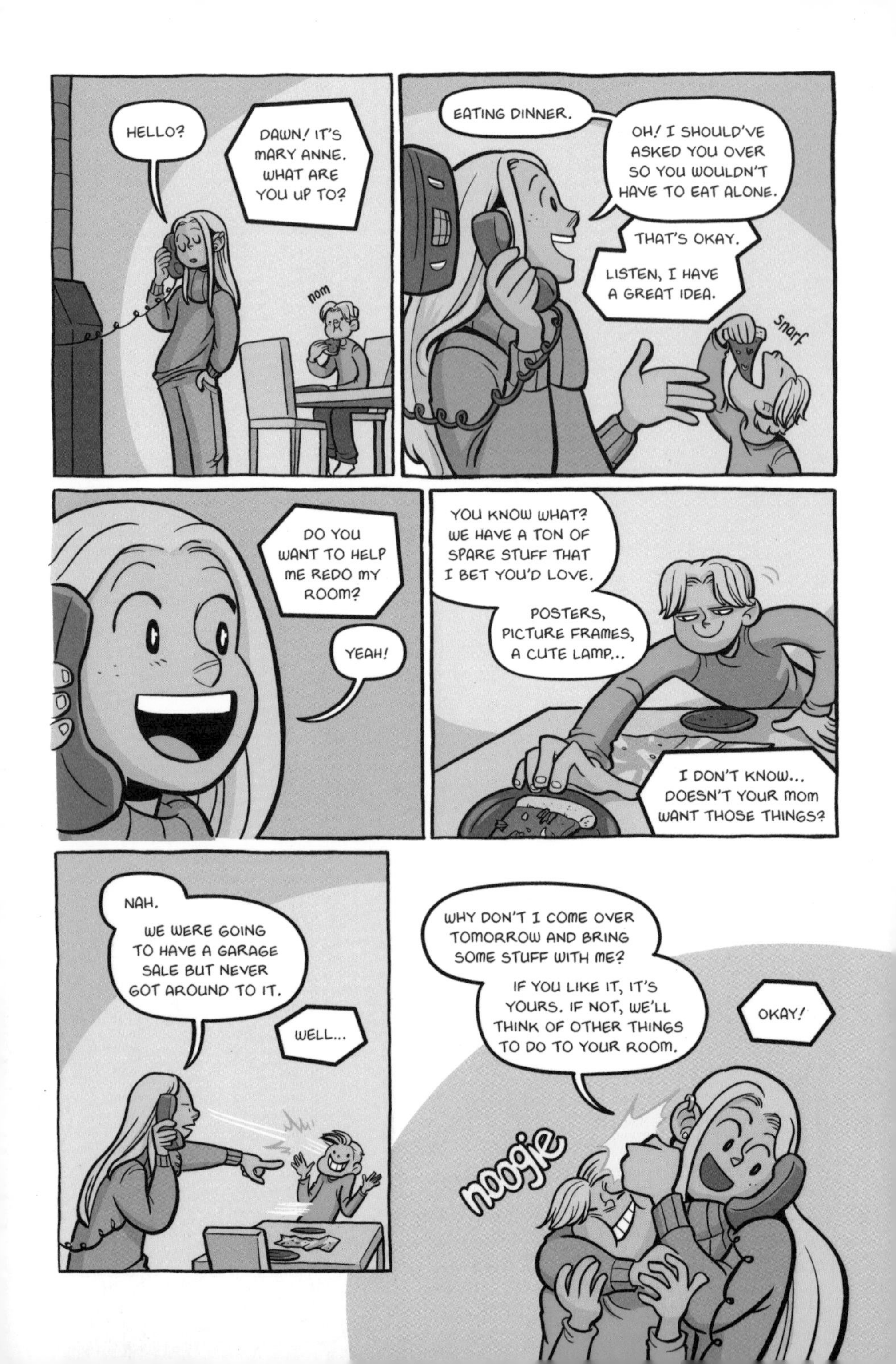
HELLO?
DAWN! IT'S MARY ANNE. WHAT ARE YOU UP TO?
nom
EATING DINNER.
OH! I SHOULD'VE ASKED YOU OVER SO YOU WOULDN'T HAVE TO EAT ALONE.
THAT'S OKAY.
LISTEN, I HAVE A GREAT IDEA.
snarf
DO YOU WANT TO HELP ME REDO MY ROOM?
YEAH!
YOU KNOW WHAT? WE HAVE A TON OF SPARE STUFF THAT I BET YOU'D LOVE.
POSTERS, PICTURE FRAMES, A CUTE LAMP...
I DON'T KNOW... DOESN'T YOUR MOM WANT THOSE THINGS?
NAH.
WE WERE GOING TO HAVE A GARAGE SALE BUT NEVER GOT AROUND TO IT.
WELL...
WHY DON'T I COME OVER TOMORROW AND BRING SOME STUFF WITH ME?
IF YOU LIKE IT, IT'S YOURS. IF NOT, WE'LL THINK OF OTHER THINGS TO DO TO YOUR ROOM.
OKAY!
noogie

THE NEXT DAY, I WENT THROUGH THE ATTIC AND FOUND SO MUCH STUFF THAT MOM HAD TO DRIVE ME OVER TO THE SPIERS'.

THIS WAS A LITTLE SNEAKY ON MY PART, SINCE IT SERVED THREE PURPOSES.
ONE, I GOT A RIDE...
TWO, WHEN MARY ANNE SAW MY MOM, SHE'D KNOW IT WAS OKAY TO USE OUR THINGS...
I'D LOVE TO SEE THESE GO TO GOOD USE.
THANKS A LOT, MRS. SCHAFER. THIS IS SO NICE OF YOU.

AND THREE, IT WOULD GIVE US A CHANCE TO SEE HOW THE BIG DATE WENT.
OH! SHARON!
GOODNESS, LET ME HELP YOU WITH THAT.
YOU'RE MAKING ME LOOK BAD! AT LEAST PRETEND IT WEIGHS **SOMETHING.**
LUGGING AROUND PAPERWORK ALL DAY **DOES** HAVE ITS BENEFITS.
hee hee
hee hee

WHERE DO WE START?
UMMM...
LET'S SEE WHAT THESE ARE! I DON'T EVEN REMEMBER.
OH! LONDON AT NIGHT! HOW PRETTY.
AND...MY DAD'S ASTRONOMY CHART?
IT'S NICE, BUT I DON'T KNOW IF IT'S ME.
HEY, YOU GUYS! WHAT ARE YOU DOING?
OKAY IF I ASK HER OVER?
SURE.
HEY, KRISTY! WE'RE REDECORATING MY ROOM! WANT TO COME OVER?
OOOOKAY.

HI. WHAT'S ALL THIS STUFF?
DAWN BROUGHT IT OVER.
DAD'S LETTING ME TAKE THE OLD STUFF OFF MY WALLS AND PUT UP WHATEVER I WANT!

HE'S LETTING YOU PUT THUMBTACKS IN THE WALLS?
I GUESS SO.
HOW COME YOU DIDN'T TELL ME YOU WERE GOING TO START REDECORATING?
I DON'T KNOW...
HEY, DID I TELL YOU? OUR PARENTS WENT ON ANOTHER DATE LAST NIGHT...
A SPONTANEOUS ONE.
OH...THAT'S COOL, I GUESS.
YOU KNOW...

I MIGHT HAVE SOME THINGS YOU COULD USE, TOO.
REMEMBER WHEN WE MADE THAT POSTER FOR ART CLASS AND IT WON THE PRIZE?
YOU STILL *HAVE* THAT?
AND I BET WE COULD USE WATSON'S STENCIL KIT TO FIX UP YOUR OLD PINK PHOTO FRAMES!
OH, WHAT A **WONDERFUL** IDEA!
AND WITH ALL OF THESE FREE DECORATIONS, GOSH!
MAYBE I *CAN* CONVINCE DAD TO REPLACE THE BEDSPREAD.
HEY, KRISTY, DO YOU REMEMBER THE TIME...
AFTER THAT, THE THREE OF US WORKED ON MARY ANNE'S ROOM FOR HOURS. WE TALKED AND PLANNED AND LAUGHED.
BUT I NOTICED TWO THINGS:
KRISTY ONLY SPOKE DIRECTLY TO MARY ANNE...
AND KRISTY NEVER LAUGHED AT MY JOKES. (EVEN THOUGH MARY ANNE DID.)

I THOUGHT KRISTY AND I HAD SMOOTHED EVERYTHING OVER WHEN SHE MADE ME AN OFFICIAL ALTERNATE OFFICER OF THE BABY-SITTERS CLUB...
BUT I GUESS I WAS WRONG.

CHAPTER 4
BEFORE I KNEW IT, THE TIME HAD COME FOR MY FIRST OFFICIAL BABY-SITTING JOB WITH THE BARRETTS.
ding dong
creeeeeak
HI, SUZI. I'm DAWN. I FIXED YOUR KNEE, REMEMBER?
nod
WELL, I'm GOING TO BABY-SIT FOR YOU TODAY.
IS YOUR mOm HOME?
nod
AND SO, I DEFEATED ANOTHER STUDENT...
mAY I COME IN?
nod
OF THE NOTORIOUS SCHOOL OF NODS.

HELLO?
ZIP
YAH! YAH!
BANG BANG BANG!

ZOW!
YOU'RE BURNED! YOU'RE A GONER!
NO, I'M DAWN, YOUR SITTER. WE MET AT THE PIKES'.
I DON'T LIKE GUNS. SO NO GUNS WHEN I'M AROUND.
AWWWWW.

OH, IS THIS MARNIE?
YEAH.

HI, MARNIE. YOU SURE ARE CU--

WHOOF.

DO YOU KNOW WHERE YOUR MOM KEEPS THE DIAPERS?
shrug

IT WAS ABOUT THEN THAT I NOTICED...

THIS PLACE WAS A **MESS!!**

tmp
tmp
tmp
DAWN? DAWN, IS THAT YOU?
HI, MRS. BARRETT.

WHERE DO YOU KEEP YOUR–
SO LONG, DARLINGS. BE GOOD FOR DAWN.

WAIT! WHERE ARE YOU GOING TO BE?
AT A JOB INTERVIEW. AND I'M LATE.

WHAT IF THERE'S AN EMERGENCY? HOW DO I REACH YOU?
CALL THE PIKES, OKAY?
WELL...

ALL RIGHT.
SCREEEEEEEE

USUALLY, I GET SOME KIND OF SPECIAL INSTRUCTION.

SNACK TIME AT 4, NO TV BEFORE HOMEWORK...

SOMETHING.

WELL...HOW WOULD YOU LIKE TO PLAY A GAME?

YEAH!!

I'M GOING TO TIME US TO SEE HOW FAST WE CAN CLEAN UP THE LIVING ROOM.
TAKE ANYTHING THAT DOESN'T BELONG IN THERE AND PUT IT WHERE IT **DOES** BELONG.
TIDY EVERYTHING ELSE UP, BUT BE CAREFUL.
DON'T WORK SO FAST YOU BREAK SOMETHING.
WE'LL HAVE TO ADD TIME TO OUR SCORE IF THAT HAPPENS.
TAKE YOUR MARKS.
GET SET.
GO!!

SIX MINUTES AND SEVENTEEN SECONDS!
IS...IS THAT A RECORD?!
IT MIGHT BE...
BUT NOT IF WE CLEAN UP THE KITCHEN EVEN FASTER!

THIS SURE IS NICER, ISN'T IT?
YEAH!
EVEN THOUGH WE DIDN'T BEAT THE RECORD THIS TIME.

HEY, DAWN?
YEAH?

DO YOU HAVE A DADDY?

WELL...YES. BUT NOT HERE. HE DOESN'T LIVE WITH US.
YEAH. HE'S IN CALIFORNIA. THREE THOUSAND MILES AWAY.
REALLY?
MY MOM AND DAD ARE DIVORCED.

SO ARE OURS.

I WONDER HOW LONG DIVORCE LASTS.
IT'S FOREVER.
THAT'S WHAT MOMMY SAID, BUT...
BUT YOU KEEP HOPING YOUR DAD WILL COME BACK?
YEAH.
YEAH.
ME TOO...
EXCEPT I KNOW HE WON'T.
hug

YOU. ARE. A.
LIAR!
A LIAR.
SUZI!
SHE REALLY THINKS DADDY'S GOING TO COME HOME FOR GOOD ONE DAY.

IF I HAD ONLY KNOWN HOW OFTEN "ANY TIME" WAS GOING TO BE, I MIGHT NOT HAVE SPOKEN SO QUICKLY.

CHAPTER 5

THE FIRST TIME I MET MARY ANNE, SHE WAS SITTING AT A CAFETERIA TABLE ALL BY HERSELF. THE BABY-SITTERS CLUB HAD JUST HAD A HUGE FIGHT.

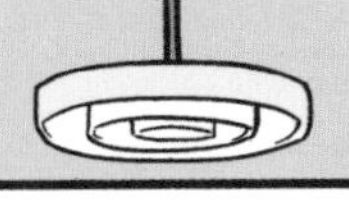
THEY WERE ALL SITTING WITH OTHER FRIENDS -- EXCEPT FOR MARY ANNE.

THAT'S WHERE I CAME IN.
milk

NOW THAT SHE AND KRISTY ARE FRIENDS AGAIN...

THEY'VE GONE BACK TO SITTING AT THEIR USUAL TABLE WITH THE SHILLABER TWINS.

HEY, GUYS.
SO??
ANY UPDATES?
MY DAD AND DAWN'S MOM WENT OUT ON **TWO** MORE DATES THIS WEEKEND.
THEY **DID?!**
WHERE'D THEY GO?
OUT TO DINNER AND THE MOVIES ON SATURDAY NIGHT...
AND THEN TO BRUNCH THE VERY NEXT MORNING.
EEEEEE!
YOU KNOW, IF YOUR PARENTS GET MARRIED...

YOU TWO...
WILL BE STEPSISTERS.

SUDDENLY, I KNEW.

KRISTY DIDN'T DISLIKE ME.
...AND THEY'LL GET MARRIED AND HAVE A BIG, BEAUTIFUL WEDDING, WITH TONS OF FLOWERS...
AND A HUUUGE CAKE!
SHE WAS JUST AFRAID OF BEING LEFT OUT.

HEY, UM, KRISTY.
AREN'T YOUR MOM AND WATSON PLANNING TO GET MARRIED SOON?

UM...YEAH. IN THE FALL, PROBABLY.
AND THEN YOU'LL HAVE A LITTLE STEPSISTER AND STEPBROTHER, RIGHT?
RIGHT. PLUS MY THREE BROTHERS.
GOSH, YOU'RE GOING TO BE A BIG FAMILY.
YEAH! FOUR BROTHERS AND YOUR FIRST SISTER.
HOW'S EVERYBODY GOING TO FIT IN YOUR HOUSE?
OH, WELL...

WE'RE... SORT OF MOVING.
TO WATSON'S MANSION.

OOOOH, A REAL **MANSION?**
A REAL MANSION.
IT'S **HUGE.**

DO YOU GET TO REDECORATE YOUR ROOM? LIKE, HOWEVER YOU WANT?
I GUESS. BUT WHAT I REALLY WANT IS EXACTLY WHAT'S IN MY ROOM RIGHT NOW.
WHAAAAT? YOU'VE HAD THAT FOR **YEARS.**

JUST THINK! YOU COULD PROBABLY DO ANYTHING YOU WANTED TO YOUR NEW ROOM.
SPORTS THEMED...
YOUR FAVORITE COLORS...
OR EVEN SOMETHING HIGH TECH --
WHAT I **WANT** IS WHAT I'VE GOT.

SO LAY OFF, OKAY?
OKAY!
SEE YOU GUYS LATER.
LATER.

...SHE DOESN'T WANT TO MOVE.
OH.
OH.
NO MATTER HOW HARD I TRIED...

IT WAS PRETTY CLEAR THAT I WAS STILL THE NEW KID.

CHAPTER 6
brrringgggg
NNNNNNG
YESSSSS.
SATURDAY MORNING. I WAS HEADED TO MY SECOND BABY-SITTING JOB FOR THE BARRETTS.
AND WE WERE FINALLY GETTING A DAY OFF FROM THIS YEAR'S RIDICULOUSLY LONG WINTER.
SUNSHINE! WARMTH! WE COULD PLAY OUTSIDE... CATCH SOME RAYS...
ding dong
MAYBE EVEN --

DAWN! GOOD MORNING! EMERGENCY NUMBER ON THE FRIDGE --
GOT TO RUN --
I'LL SEE YOU TONIGHT!!
whoosh

HOW LONG ARE YOU STAYING?
WHAT'S FOR BREAKFAST?
MOH?
UH --

ring ring
HOLD THOSE THOUGHTS.

HELLO, BARRETT RESIDENCE.
DAAAAAWN!

CLAUDIA? IS THAT YOU?
YEAH!
STACEY, MALLORY, AND I ARE SITTING FOR THE PIKES -- ALL OF THEM -- AND WE'RE THINKING ABOUT HAVING A PICNIC.

WHAT TIME?
LET'S SAY... 1:00?
WE'LL DO LUNCH, YOU BRING SNACKS?

YEAH! PERFECT.
BUT WE'D NEED TO HUSTLE!

9:00 - Breakfast.

9:30 - Clean table.

10:00 - Kids
get dressed.

10:30 - Straighten
bedrooms.

11:00 - Still
straightening rooms.

11:30 - Snacks
for picnic??
AHA!
Mix

12:00 - ~~Playtime~~
Clean kitchen.
POMF
Flour

12:30 - Brownies!

12:50 - Head
over to picnic!

STACEY.
PSSSST. STACEY.
DAWN! YOU MADE IT!

UH...ARE YOU OKAY?
HOW MANY PIKE KIDS ARE THERE?
EIGHT. YOU KNOW THAT.

RIGHT, AND THERE ARE THREE BARRETT KIDS.
AND YOU AND ME AND CLAUDIA.
SO... FOURTEEN.

NOW COUNT THE PEOPLE IN THE BACKYARD.

WELL, LET'S SEE. THERE'S BUDDY, SUZI, AND MARNIE...
MALLORY, BYRON, ADAM...
JORDAN, VANESSA...
NICKY, MARGO, CLAIRE...
AND JENNY PREZZIOSO??
WE MIGHT AS WELL ASK HER TO STAY.
UGHHHHH.

BZZZZZZ.
HEY!

CLAUDIA! JORDAN GAVE ME THE BIZZER SIGN!
OH NO.

WHAT?
THE PIKE KIDS MADE IT UP. IT'S LIKE... AN INSULT OR SOMETHING?

JUST IGNORE HIM.
BUT HE GAVE ME THE **BIZZER** SIGN!

BZZZZZZZZZZZZZ.

BIZZERS DON'T GET BROWNIES!!

THAT WAS A CLOSE ONE.

HEY, MARNIE.
YOU WANT A BROWNIE?
STOP!!

WHAT ARE YOU DOING?!
WHAT ARE **YOU** DOING?!

MARNIE'S **ALLERGIC.**

SHE CAN'T EAT CHOCOLATE. IT MAKES HER REALLY SICK.
WHAT...? BUT...

MRS. BARRETT NEVER TOLD ME THAT.

I APOLOGIZED TO MALLORY FOUR TIMES.
THEN I BEGAN TO FEEL ANGRY.
I KNEW MRS. BARRETT WAS GOING THROUGH A LOT RIGHT NOW, BUT...
SHE NEVER GAVE ME INSTRUCTIONS FOR THE KIDS.
SHE HARDLY PAID ATTENTION TO THEM.
WE HAD TO DO ALL OF THE HOUSEWORK.
AND HER NEGLIGENCE ALMOST HURT MARNIE.
I'M HOME!
...OH, **DAWN!!**
MRS. BARRETT --
I KNEW I NEEDED TO TALK TO HER ABOUT EVERYTHING.
OH GOODNESS, I DON'T KNOW HOW YOU DO IT.
THE HOUSE LOOKS SIMPLY INCREDIBLE, THANK YOU.

OH, UH...IT'S NOTHING.
BUT WHAT CAN YOU SAY TO SOMETHING LIKE THAT?

Wednesday, May 27th

This evning I babysat for Dawn Shafers brother Jeff. I could tell he thoght he was to old for a baby-sitter but Dawn was sitting at the Barretts and her mom had suddenly gotten tickits to a Concert and Mrs. Shaffer didnt want to leave Jeff alone at night. She called me at the last minute and luckly I was free. Sitting for Jeff was an easy job.

But! Dawn I noticed this is the second night in a row you've sat at the Baretts. And I looked in our apontment book and you were their four times last week. Maybe you are over doing it?

I am telling you this as a freind.

* Claudia *

CHAPTER 7

SORRY! GOTTA GO!
BARRETTS!
CLAUDIA WAS RIGHT.
WITH MRS. BARRETT'S DIVORCE AND JOB HUNT, IT SEEMED LIKE SHE ALWAYS NEEDED SOMEONE TO LOOK AFTER THE KIDS...
AND THEY LIKED ME BEST.
ONE TIME, I EVEN MISSED A MEETING OF THE BABY-SITTERS CLUB.
MRS. BARRETT HAD PROMISED SHE'D BE BACK BY 5:30, BUT ENDED UP STAYING OUT UNTIL 6 WITHOUT SO MUCH AS A CALL!
BUT I DID FINALLY GET UP THE NERVE TO TALK TO HER.

THANK YOU, DAWN. I DON'T KNOW WHAT I'D DO --
MRS. BARRETT?

HOW COME YOU DIDN'T TELL ME MARNIE'S ALLERGIC TO CHOCOLATE?

I...DIDN'T TELL YOU?
NO.

I ALMOST GAVE HER A PIECE OF BROWNIE THE OTHER DAY. MALLORY STOPPED ME JUST IN TIME.
MY GOODNESS!

DO THE KIDS HAVE ANY OTHER ALLERGIES?
NONE THAT WE'RE AWARE OF.

IS THERE ANYTHING ELSE I SHOULD KNOW?

JUST ONE THING. IF MY EX-HUSBAND EVER CALLS...

DON'T LET HIM **TALK** TO THE CHILDREN.
DON'T TELL HIM HE CAN **SEE** THE CHILDREN.
AND **DON'T** TELL HIM I'M OUT.

JUST SAY YOU'RE HELPING ME AND I'M BUSY. HE --
crash

EEEEK!
thnk
SUZI!

KIDS...

I'LL TAKE CARE OF IT. WHY DON'T YOU DRY SUZI OFF?

BUDDY, GO GET THE PAPER TOWELS. WE'LL CLEAN UP.
AWWW.

THANK YOU AGAIN, DAWN. I HOPE YOU KNOW HOW MUCH WE APPRECIATE YOU.
WITH EVERYTHING THAT'S BEEN GOING ON, WELL, I JUST --
hug
ring

I'LL GET IT!
BUDDY! I TOLD YOU, YOU ARE NOT TO ANSWER THE -- !

DAD SAYS WHERE ARE WE?
YOU WERE S'POSED TO DROP OFF ME AND SUZI HALF AN HOUR AGO.

OH GRACIOUS, I COMPLETELY FORGOT!!

DAWN, I'LL SEE YOU WEDNESDAY!

SO THAT DIDN'T REALLY GO AS PLANNED.

IT'S BEEN A FEW WEEKS NOW, AND LIKE CLAUDIA SAID, I'VE BEEN SITTING FOR THE BARRETTS A **LOT.**

IT'S STARTING TO FEEL LIKE I'M, I DON'T KNOW, A STAND-IN MOM.
BUDDY? WHAT'S THE MATTER?
sniffle

M-MY HOMEWORK.
WELL, CAN I HELP? I'M PRETTY SMART.

I NEED **MOM'S** HELP.

I'M SUPPOSED TO ASK HER ABOUT OUR FAMILY TREE, BUT SHE'S ALWAYS BUSY.
OR TIRED.
AND I REALLY WANT IT TO BE GOOD.
WELL, LET'S DO AS MUCH AS WE CAN, OKAY?
IT TOOK A WHILE, BUT AFTER ASKING BUDDY A LOT OF QUESTIONS AND MAKING SOME PHONE CALLS TO MRS. PIKE...
WE FIGURED OUT WHERE BUDDY'S RELATIVES BELONGED ON THE TREE.
ALL **HE'D** HAVE TO DO WAS GET THE MISSING NAMES FROM HIS MOM.

THAT WASN'T THE WORST I HAD TO DEAL WITH, THOUGH.
URGHHHHHHH.

HWORKKK

AH!

WHERE IS IT, WHERE IS IT...

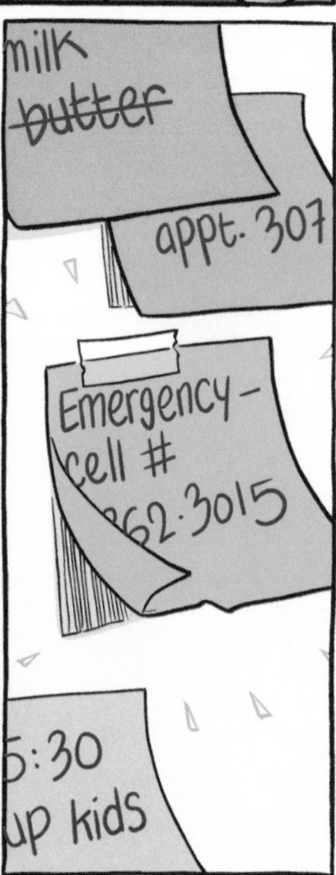
milk
butter
appt. 307
Emergency - cell #
62-3015
5:30
up kids

ring
ring

HI! I'M AWAY FROM MY PHONE RIGHT NOW, BUT LEAVE YOUR NAME AND NUMBER...

HER PHONE WAS OFF.
SHE ALWAYS FORGETS TO TURN IT ON.
hrrrr rrrkk

wahhhhh
hwork!

wahhhhhh
hworkkkk

HELLO?

MALLORY! THANK YOU SO MUCH FOR COMING.
SUZI'S BEEN THROWING UP AND I CAN'T GET AHOLD OF MRS. BARRETT. COULD YOU...?
I'M ON IT.

I SPENT THE REST OF THE DAY READING TO SUZI IN THE BATHROOM...

WHILE MALLORY TOOK CARE OF MARNIE AND BUDDY.

beep
toktoktok

WHAT'S GOTTEN INTO YOU?

hrrrrkkkk
BOTH MY FAMILY AND MALLORY'S ENDED UP CATCHING THAT BUG.

CHAPTER 8

ding dong
BUDDY? WHAT ARE YOU DOING HERE?
WEEEELL...
Great Great G'pa Don
Great Great G'ma Na
Great Grandpa Bill
Great Gran Mary Alice
Grandma Kay
Great Aunt Eva
Great Aunt Julia
Mom Natalie
Dad Hamilton
Me Buddy Barrett
WE GOT **THESE** BACK TODAY!
IT TURNED OUT GREAT.
THANKS FOR HELPING ME, DAWN.
YOU'RE WELCOME, BUDDY.

I WAS GLAD I COULD HELP, BUT BUDDY'S MOM SHOULD HAVE BEEN THE ONE HELPING HIM WITH HIS FAMILY TREE...
ding dong
sigh
BEING PROUD OF THE GOLD STAR...
HELLO, DAWN.
COME ON UPSTAIRS.
AND GETTING THE HUG.
THANKS, JANINE.

I CALL THIS MEETING OF THE BSC TO ORDER.
ANY NEW ITEMS OF BUSINESS?
I THOUGHT I HAD DING DONGS BACK HERE.
YEAH, LAST YEAR.
THAT'S **OLD** BUSINESS!
I HAVE SOMETHING.
OH?
I JUST WANTED TO SAY...
MALLORY'S BEEN DOING A GREAT JOB.

MARNIE WOULD HAVE BEEN IN SERIOUS TROUBLE IF MAL HADN'T BEEN AT THE PICNIC.
GOOD JOB, MALLORY!
AND SHE WAS REALLY HELPFUL WHEN SUZI GOT SICK.
TH-THANKS.
AND YOU KNOW...
I DIDN'T HAVE TO PASS YOUR CRAZY TEST TO DO IT.
HOLD ON JUST A --
ACTUALLY, YOU'RE RIGHT.
WE DID HAVE TO DO AN AWFUL LOT OF RESEARCH OURSELVES TO PUT THAT TOGETHER.
AND I **STILL** COULDN'T REMEMBER EVERYTHING.
WELL...

YOU GUYS MAKE A GOOD POINT.
AND MALLORY HAS BEEN REALLY HELPFUL, EVEN BEFORE WE INVITED HER TO JOIN THE CLUB.
rustle
IN THAT CASE...
gumm
Pretzsies
HOW ABOUT A TASTY TOAST FOR OUR NEW JUNIOR MEMBER?
TO MALLORY!

THE REST OF THE MEETING WAS PRETTY NORMAL, UNTIL...

OH, BEFORE I FORGET...

KRISTY, I WANTED TO ASK YOU ABOUT SOMETHING.
WHAT?

I WAS BABY-SITTING FOR DAVID MICHAEL THE OTHER DAY...
YEAH, I REMEMBER.

UM...
STACEY?
Pant pant

WHEN YOU MOVED, DID THEY PACK UP **EVERYTHING** IN THE VAN?
OH, OF COURSE. EVERY LAST THING.

THEY DIDN'T LEAVE **ANYTHING** BEHIND.

E-EVEN YOUR PETS??
???

SNUFFLE

OH, DAVID MICHAEL!
THEY WON'T PUT **LOUIE** IN THE VAN.

hahahaha
DAVID MICHAEL!

BUT TALKING TO HIM GOT ME THINKING.

WHAT ARE WE GOING TO DO ABOUT THE CLUB WHEN YOU MOVE?

IT'S ONLY A FEW MILES AWAY --
MOM WON'T LET ME BIKE HERE FROM WATSON'S.

COULD WE MEET SOMEWHERE ELSE?
BUT WE'D NEED A PHONE.
OUR CLIENTS HAVE TO KNOW WHERE TO REACH US.

STUPID, STUPID WATSON.
HEY, DON'T GET DOWN ON WATSON. IT'S NOT HIS FAULT.
IT'S NOT ANYBODY'S FAULT.

A LOT **YOU** KNOW.

I MAY KNOW MORE THAN YOU THINK.
YOU'RE NOT THE ONLY ONE WHOSE PARENTS GOT DIVORCED.

NO, BUT I'M THE ONLY ONE WHOSE MOM CHOSE TO GET MARRIED TO A GUY WHO'S SO RICH HE LIVES OVER ON **MILLIONAIRE'S LANE.**

AND **I'M** THE ONLY ONE WHO MAY HAVE TO DROP OUT OF THE CLUB. THE CLUB **I** STARTED.
KRISTY!

WE COULDN'T RUN THE CLUB WITHOUT YOU. IT WOULDN'T BE RIGHT.

NO KRISTY...
NO CLUB.

CHAPTER 9

MOM, THIS MIGHT BE THE FIRST PICNIC EVER ATTENDED BY PEOPLE IN DOWN JACKETS.

FOR PITY'S SAKE, DAWN. IT'S LOVELY OUT.

OF COURSE, MOST PEOPLE ALREADY HAD PLANS. IN THE END, THE ONLY ONES WHO COULD MAKE IT WERE MY GRANDPARENTS, THE SPIERS, THE BARRETTS...

DO YOU THINK I COULD SUBSTITUTE RAW HONEY FOR SUGAR?
UM...
AND KRISTY AND DAVID MICHAEL.

WHAT IF, INSTEAD OF TRYING TO MAKE ALL THIS FANCY STUFF, WE JUST DO HAMBURGERS, HOT DOGS, AND POTATO SALAD?
HOT DOGS! DO YOU EVEN KNOW WHAT'S IN A --

WE'RE IN CONNECTICUT NOW, MOM.
PEOPLE **BARBECUE** THINGS HERE. WE SHOULD TRY TO SERVE FOOD THEY'LL EAT.

WELL, I SUPPOSE YOUR GRANDPA'S VERY GOOD WITH THE GRILL.
AND IT'LL BE SO **EASY.**
THEY EVEN HAVE READY-MADE POTATO SALAD AT THE GROCERY STORE.
LET'S GO!
AS WE SHOPPED, I REMEMBERED SOMETHING.
UH, MOM?
DIDN'T YOUR PARENTS NOT LIKE MR. SPIER?
THAT WAS A LONG TIME AGO...
I HOPE.

SOON...

KEEP AN EYE ON THEM. THIS IS A GOOD CHANCE TO SEE HOW THEY'RE DOING.
AND WHETHER OR NOT YOUR GRANDPARENTS STILL DISAPPROVE OF MY DAD.
WE MIGHT HAVE TO AVERT A **CRISIS.**
HEY...

MARY ANNE...
WHERE ARE YOUR FATHER'S GLASSES??
HE GOT CONTACTS.
YOUR **FATHER?**
I DON'T BELIEVE IT. THIS IS TOO MUCH.
flop
haha
ha

COME AND GET IT!
SO, RICHARD, HOW ARE THINGS AT THOMPSON, THOMPSON, AND ABRAMS?
WELL, I HAVEN'T BEEN WITH THEM IN QUITE SOME TIME.
OH?
I STARTED MY OWN FIRM ABOUT FOUR YEARS AGO.
OH?
AND ARE YOU STILL LIVING ON TAYLOR STREET?
WHY, NO! WE'RE OVER AT BRADFORD COURT NOW.
OH! WHAT A LOVELY AREA.

I'M GLAD EVERYTHING TURNED OUT OKAY.
YEAH.
YOUR PARENTS REALLY LIKE EACH OTHER.

YOU MIGHT ACTUALLY END UP BEING SISTERS.

KRISTY...
ARE YOU ALL RIGHT?

I...
WELL, YOU KNOW.

MY MOM GETTING MARRIED, AND THE MOVE AND ALL. IT'S A LOT.

I'M GOING TO BE SO FAR AWAY FROM YOU GUYS, AND I DON'T KNOW WHAT'S HAPPENING WITH THE CLUB...

sniffle

YOU DON'T WANT TO BE LEFT BEHIND.

WHEN WE MOVED HERE, WE HAD TO LEAVE A LOT BEHIND.
OUR HOUSE, OUR COUSINS AND BEST FRIENDS, DAD...
THEY'RE ALL THOUSANDS OF MILES AWAY NOW.

BUT WE STILL TALK ALL THE TIME.

YOU'RE ONLY MOVING ACROSS TOWN.
DO YOU REALLY THINK WE'RE GOING TO LET OUR FRIENDSHIP CHANGE OVER A FEW MILES?

hug
OF COURSE NOT.

Tuesday, June 2

This afternoon I baby-sat for Buddy, Suzi, and Marnie Barrett. What a time I had! I don't know if it's the weather or problems with the divorce or what, but the kids were wild. Wild and cranky. I'm sure the sitter they really wanted was Dawn. I don't know how you handle them, Dawn. I hope they behave better for you than they do for me.

By the way, there was a really strange phone call from Mr. Barrett today, wanting to know where Buddy was. I wouldn't give him any information. When I told Mrs. Barrett about the call, she turned purple (not really) and said he shouldn't have called when he knew darn well she'd be out. What's going on?

I think we should all be careful of calls from Mr. Barrett.

Mary Anne

CHAPTER 10

TODAY, FOR THE FIRST TIME IN AGES, I WASN'T THE ONE BABY-SITTING FOR THE BARRETTS.
I DIDN'T ENVY MARY ANNE -- IT HAD BEEN RAINING FOR THREE DAYS STRAIGHT.
PEW!
PEW!

I GOT YOU! YOU'RE DEAD!
WELL, I'M NOT DEAD FOR LONG, BECAUSE I'M COMING INTO YOUR HOUSE.
STAND ASIDE, MARTIAN MAN.

MARTIAN?! I'M A COWBOY! FROM VENUS!
THIS IS OBVIOUSLY A VENUS WEAPON!
DAWN?

BIZZ.

WAHH HHH

WAHHHHHHH

HI, MARY ANNE!
wahhhh
DON'T FORGET MARNIE'S ALLERGIC TO CHOCOLAAAAATE!

ALL RIGHT, WHO WANTS TO --

BIZZ

wahhhhhhhhhh

BUDDY, YOU GIVE ONE MORE BIZZER SIGN TO ANYONE TODAY -- **ANYONE** -- AND YOU'LL HAVE TO STAY IN YOUR ROOM UNTIL YOUR MOTHER COMES HOME.
WILL **NOT.**

YES, YOU WILL. I'M IN CHARGE HERE, AND WHAT I SAY GOES.
WILL YOU TELL MOM IF I'M BAD?

I MIGHT.
TATTLETALE!

THAT'S THE WAY IT IS.

NOW. YOU KNOW WHAT WE'RE GOING TO DO TODAY?

NOT READ.
NOT COLOR.
NOT WATCH TV.
NOT PLAY *CANDY LAND.*

NOPE. I CAN TELL YOU'RE TIRED OF THE SAME OLD RAINY-DAY STUFF.

SO TODAY WE'RE GOING TO GO OUTSIDE FOR A **PUDDLE WALK.**

JUMP IN AS MANY PUDDLES AS YOU CAN.
TRY TO MAKE BIG SPLASHES!

aaaaAAA
AAAACK!
sploosh

HE **SPLASHED** ME!
GOOD!

YOU'RE WEARING YOUR SWIMSUIT AND RAINCOAT.
THESE CLOTHES ARE **SUPPOSED** TO GET WET.

OHHHHHHHH.

PKEWWWWWW!
sploosh
YA-HAAAA!
splsh
splsh

splish

tmp
tmp
giggle

OKAY, LET'S JUST LEAVE OUR FLIP-FLOPS BY THE --
ring
ring

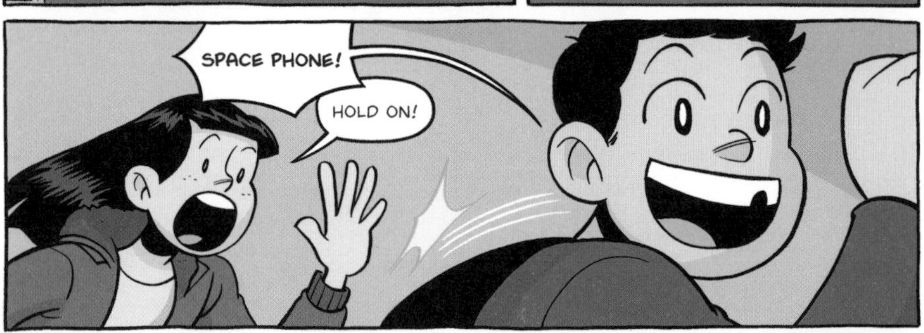
SPACE PHONE!
HOLD ON!

NOOOOO! VENUS NEEDS ME!
HELLO, BARRETT RESIDENCE.

BZZZZZZ
BUDDY!
I TOLD YOU WHAT WOULD HAPPEN IF YOU DID THAT AGAIN.

GO TO YOUR ROOM.

SORRY ABOUT THAT. HELLO?
HELLO? WHO'S THIS?
stomp
stomp

THIS IS MARY ANNE SPIER, THE SITTER. WHO'S THIS?
THIS IS MR. BARRETT.

WOULD YOU MIND PUTTING BUDDY ON?
OR SUZI?

I'M SORRY, THEY'RE...AT A FRIEND'S HOUSE.
OH, FINE.

Slam
beep
beep
beep

WHEN MRS. BARRETT GOT HOME, THERE WAS QUITE THE SCENE.
BUDDY WAS MAD BECAUSE HE'D BEEN PUNISHED...
MRS. BARRETT WAS MAD BECAUSE BUDDY HAD MISBEHAVED...
AND SHE WAS **VERY** UPSET THAT MR. BARRETT HAD CALLED.

HE'S ONLY SUPPOSED TO SPEAK TO THE KIDS ON ALTERNATING TUESDAYS, AND THIS IS THE WRONG DAY.
IT'S PART OF THE CUSTODY ARRANGEMENT, AND HE CAN'T KEEP HIS OWN **SCHEDULE** STRAIGHT!

AND BUDDY, WHAT IS THE **MATTER** WITH YOU?
I GET NOTES FROM YOUR TEACHER, YOU GIVE MARY ANNE TROUBLE...

I DON'T HAVE **TIME** FOR THIS, YOUNG MAN.
I CANNOT BE YOUR MOTHER AND FATHER, RUN THIS HOUSEHOLD, LOOK FOR A JOB...

AND STRAIGHTEN OUT THE MESSES YOU GET YOURSELF INTO.

IT'S TOO MUCH TO ASK OF ANYBODY.

CHAPTER 11

THE RAIN DIDN'T LET UP AFTER THAT.

tptptptptp
I DIDN'T REALLY MIND. IT MADE ME THINK OF THE RAINY SEASON IN CALIFORNIA.
PLUS, MY MOM WAS IN A GREAT MOOD.

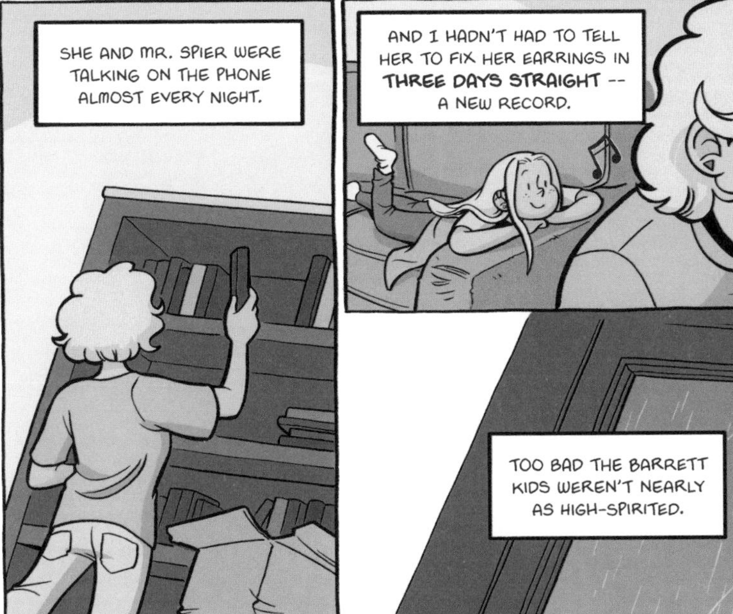
SHE AND MR. SPIER WERE TALKING ON THE PHONE ALMOST EVERY NIGHT.
AND I HADN'T HAD TO TELL HER TO FIX HER EARRINGS IN **THREE DAYS STRAIGHT** -- A NEW RECORD.
TOO BAD THE BARRETT KIDS WEREN'T NEARLY AS HIGH-SPIRITED.

HOW ABOUT... PUTTING ON A PLAY?
NOOOOOOO.

MAKING OUR OWN COMIC BOOK?
TOO HARD.

WELL, WHAT DO **YOU** WANT TO DO?
I DUNNOOOOOO.

sigh.

tp
HEY!
THE RAIN STOPPED!
LET'S GO **OUTSIDE!**

WAIT!

HOLD ON A SEC. WE'VE GOTTA BE SMART.

BUDDY, YOU'RE READY AS SOON AS YOU PUT ON YOUR BOOTS.
SO YOU CAN GO AHEAD.

BUT, SUZI AND MARNIE, IT'S CHILLY OUT TODAY. WE HAVE TO GET YOU BUNDLED UP FIRST.
NO FAIR!!

IT'LL ONLY BE A MINUTE. BUDDY, BOOTS AND JACKET.
OKAYYYY!
grumble

wehhhh
SOUNDS LIKE A DIAPER.
GOOD TIMING, MARNIE!
weh
shoop

HOPE BUDDY'S READY FOR THIS!
BUDDY?

BUDDY?

BUDDY?

BUDDY?
BUDDYYYY!

BUDDY? NO, HE HASN'T BEEN BY.
I WAS HOPING HE'D COME SEE MY NEW WALKIE-TALKIES, THOUGH.

TRY CALLING THE MURPHYS. AND THE SPENCERS.
AND LET ME KNOW IF YOU DON'T FIND HIM IN ABOUT HALF AN HOUR.

WHERE ON EARTH COULD BUDDY HAVE GONE?
WHEN WE GOT BACK, WE CHECKED THE YARD AND HOUSE ONE MORE TIME, AND THEN I STARTED MAKING CALLS.
I CALLED THE MURPHYS AND THE SPENCERS, LIKE MRS. PIKE SUGGESTED, AND THEN FOUR MORE NEIGHBORS WHOSE NUMBERS MR. MURPHY GAVE ME.
IF YOU SEE HIM, COULD YOU LET ME KNOW?
UH-HUH.
THANK YOU.

TO MAKE MATTERS WORSE, I COULDN'T GET AHOLD OF MRS. BARRETT.
HI! I CAN'T COME TO THE PHONE RIGHT NOW, BUT --
CLICK
BUDDY WAS MY RESPONSIBILITY, AND I'D LET HIM DOWN.

AFTER THAT, I CALLED MRS. PIKE BACK IN A PANIC.
SHE TOLD ME NOT TO WORRY, AND WE STARTED ASKING PEOPLE TO HELP LOOK FOR HIM.
ALL RIGHT, EVERYONE!
SPREAD OUT AND LOOK FOR BUDDY. GO IN PAIRS OR GROUPS OF THREE.
YOUNGER CHILDREN, GO WITH AN ADULT.
DAWN AND I WILL STAY BY THE PHONE IN CASE BUDDY CALLS.
COME BACK HERE IF YOU HAVE ANYTHING TO REPORT.

WHY HASN'T SOMEONE FOUND HIM BY NOW? HOW FAR COULD HE HAVE GOTTEN?
I DON'T KNOW, SWEETIE, BUT HE'LL TURN UP.
WHAT IF HE'S HURT? WHAT IF HE CLIMBED A TREE AND FELL OUT?
OR GOT HIT BY A CAR? I COULDN'T --
ring ring
HELLO? BARRETT RESIDENCE --
BUDDY, IS THAT YOU??
DON'T HANG UP! YOU'VE BEEN SELECTED TO RECEIVE A SPECIAL
AAAGH!
ding dong
JUST CHECKING IN. NO NEWS FROM HIGH STREET OR SLATE STREET.

scribble
tok tok tok
HEY, DAWN. HEY, MOM.
THE DOOR WAS OPEN.

I GOT YOUR NOTE AND CAME OVER LIKE YOU SAID TO. WHAT'S GOING ON?
HONEY, BUDDY'S MISSING. EVERYONE'S OUT LOOKING. HAVE YOU SEEN HIM?
SURE I HAVE. AND HE'S NOT MISSING.

WHAT? WHERE IS HE??
HE'S AT HIS LESSON.
HUH?

SUZI, DOES BUDDY TAKE ANY KIND OF LESSONS? LIKE PIANO OR ART?
UH...

NO...?

HONEY, WHAT MAKES YOU THINK BUDDY IS AT A LESSON?
WELL...

AT THE SAME TIME MRS. KATZ AND SANDY PICKED ME UP FOR MY PIANO LESSON...
I SAW SOMEONE PICK BUDDY UP.
SO I THOUGHT...

YOU SAW BUDDY GET INTO A CAR WITH SOMEONE THIS MORNING?

nod

I'M GOING TO CALL THE POLICE.

BUDDY!
BUDDYYYYYY...!!

CHAPTER 12

DO YOU REMEMBER ANYTHING ELSE ABOUT THE CAR?
UM...
DID YOU SEE THE LICENSE PLATE? THE DRIVER?
POLICE

I DON'T...
WAS IT A MAN OR A WOMAN?

I DON'T **KNOW**, OKAY?

WE LIVE THREE HOUSES AWAY, AND BESIDES, I WASN'T PAYING ATTENTION.
I DIDN'T THINK THERE WAS ANY **REASON** TO.

MRS. KATZ PICKED ME UP, AND I SAW BUDDY GET INTO A CAR IN HIS DRIVEWAY. THAT'S **ALL.**
BUT YOU'RE SURE IT WAS A BLUE CAR.
YEAH.

A BLUE CAR.
AND YOU DIDN'T NOTICE THE DRIVER.
NO.

DID BUDDY LOOK SCARED AS HE GOT IN THE CAR? LIKE HE DIDN'T WANT TO GO?
NO. HE WAS OPENING THE DOOR AND GETTING IN.

DID YOU RECOGNIZE THE CAR? HAVE YOU SEEN IT AROUND HERE BEFORE?
I...

I DON'T KNOW. IT WAS JUST A CAR.

ANY MORE QUESTIONS?
JUST A COUPLE.

JORDAN, I KNOW WE'VE ASKED YOU THIS BEFORE.
BUT ARE YOU **POSITIVE** YOU DIDN'T SEE THE DRIVER? NOT EVEN WHETHER IT WAS A MAN OR A WOMAN?
I WAS LOOKING AT **BUDDY,** NOT THE DRIVER.

ONE LAST THING.
ABOUT WHAT TIME DID YOU SEE BUDDY GET INTO THE CAR?

MOM, WHAT TIME DID MRS. KATZ PICK ME UP?
11:15, HONEY.

11:15, THEN. MY PIANO LESSON WAS AT 11:30.
scribble

AS FOR ME, THE POLICE MOSTLY HAD QUESTIONS ABOUT MR. BARRETT.
THEY SEEMED DISAPPOINTED WHEN I SAID I DIDN'T KNOW MUCH ABOUT HIM, OR HIS DIVORCE WITH MRS. BARRETT...

BUT THEY WERE **VERY** INTERESTED WHEN THEY FOUND OUT THAT MRS. BARRETT DIDN'T WANT MR. BARRETT CALLING THE KIDS.

25
POLICE

DAWN?
MARNIE WILL BE AWAKE SOON.
I SHOULD GET BACK TO WORK.
YOU'RE A BRAVE GIRL. I'M VERY PROUD OF YOU.
SHOULD'VE SEEN ME BEFORE YOU GOT HERE.
WELL, JEFF AND I WILL BE HELPING WITH THE NEIGHBORHOOD SEARCH, SO...
JUST YELL IF YOU NEED ANYTHING.
THANKS, MOM.

FOR THE NEXT HOUR, THE POLICE CAME AND WENT.

THEY SEARCHED THE HOUSE FOR AN ADDRESS BOOK OR ANY CLUE AS TO WHERE MR. BARRETT MIGHT BE, BUT DIDN'T FIND MUCH.

MALLORY VOLUNTEERED TO LOOK AFTER SUZI AT THE PIKES' HOUSE, AND I CALLED TO SEE IF SUZI REMEMBERED WHERE HER DAD LIVED.
UM...IN HIS 'PARTMENT?

WHILE ALL OF THIS WAS GOING ON, I STILL HAD MARNIE TO LOOK AFTER.

ring
ring

HELLO?
grab!
HELLO?
DAWN?
BUDDY, IS THAT YOU?
YEAH, I --
BUDDY! WE'RE WORRIED TO DEATH. WHERE ARE YOU?
AT A GAS STATION.
A GAS STATION?? WHERE -- WHAT --
HOW DID YOU GET THERE?
WHOSE CAR? WHOSE CAR DID YOU GET INTO?
DAD'S.
BUT I DON'T THINK I'M SUPPOSED TO BE WITH HIM.
I KNEW YOU'D BE WORRIED, THOUGH, DAWN --
sffffkkkktktk
BUDDY? BUDDY?!
DAWN? HEY, HOW DOES THIS THING WORK? WE'RE ON OUR WAY HOME, OKAY? WE'RE --

AHHHH!
beep beep
yoink
THERE'S NO ONE ON THE LINE.
IT WAS BUDDY!!
HE WAS WITH HIS DAD. AT A GAS STATION.
AS DETECTIVE NORTON MADE A CALL...
boop
I BEGAN TO INDULGE IN A FANTASY.
MR. BARRETT WOULD BRING BUDDY HOME...
k-chak
EVERYONE WOULD SEE THAT EVERYTHING WAS FINE AND LEAVE...
AND MRS. BARRETT WOULD NEVER KNOW THAT ANYTHING HAD GONE WRONG.

SO YOU'RE TELLING ME THAT MY EX-HUSBAND... **TOOK**...BUDDY THIS MORNING.
AND YOU DIDN'T KNOW UNTIL **BUDDY** CALLED?

THAT'S CORRECT. I DON'T MEAN TO ALARM YOU...

BUT HAS YOUR DIVORCE BEEN A FRIENDLY ONE?
NO, IT HASN'T. WHY?

BECAUSE, WELL, A LOT OF MISSING KIDS ARE CHILDREN OF DIVORCE.
THEY'VE BEEN TAKEN BY PARENTS WHO WANT CUSTODY, BUT HAVEN'T BEEN GRANTED IT.

OH, **NO.** HAM AND I HAVE PROBLEMS, BUT HE'D NEVER **KIDNAP** THE KIDS. I MEAN, HE ALREADY GETS THEM TWICE A...

TWICE A...

scoot

flip
flip

OOPS.

20 MINUTES LATER

slam
tptptp
thud

DAWN!
BUDDY!

I'm SORRY I MADE YOU WORRY.
I'm **STARVING.** DO WE HAVE COOKIES?
LET'S SEE WHAT WE CAN FIND.

WHILE BUDDY AND I WENT ON OUR LITTLE MISSION, THE POLICE GOT THE FULL STORY OUT OF MR. BARRETT.

MRS. BARRETT HAD BEEN MIXING UP THEIR SCHEDULE A LOT, AND WHEN HE REALIZED THAT SHE HAD CONFUSED THE DATES AGAIN TODAY, HE GOT MAD.

HE DECIDED TO TEACH HER A LESSON.
HIS PLAN WAS TO COME BY, TAKE THE KIDS, AND WAIT FOR MRS. BARRETT TO FIGURE OUT HER MISTAKE.
WHEN HE SAW BUDDY ALL BY HIMSELF, HE THOUGHT IT'D BE EASIEST TO JUST TAKE HIM.
HAM83

THEY WENT TO LUNCH AND A THEME PARK, BUT BUDDY DIDN'T SEEM HAPPY.
WHEN MR. BARRETT ASKED WHAT WAS WRONG, BUDDY SAID HE WAS WORRIED ABOUT **ME**, BECAUSE I DIDN'T KNOW WHERE HE WAS.

THAT WAS WHEN MR. BARRETT REALIZED THAT HIS EX-WIFE WASN'T EVEN HOME.
AND WHO KNEW WHAT A BABY-SITTER WOULD DO WHEN SHE FOUND OUT ONE OF HER CHARGES WAS MISSING?

THE POLICE GAVE MR. BARRETT A WARNING, BUT THAT WAS IT.
THEY DID STRONGLY SUGGEST, HOWEVER, THAT THE BARRETTS TALK TO THEIR LAWYERS ABOUT THEIR CUSTODY ARRANGEMENTS.
BUT THAT WASN'T QUITE THE END OF IT.
I HAD SOMETHING TO TELL MRS. BARRETT.

CHAPTER 13
I WENT OVER THE NEXT MORNING.
MRS. BARRETT HAD SUGGESTED THAT MR. BARRETT TAKE THE KIDS FOR THE DAY, AND I'D NEVER HEARD THE HOUSE SO QUIET.
IT WAS WEIRD.
SO, DAWN, WHAT IS IT YOU WANTED TO TALK ABOUT?
WELL...
I REALLY LIKE BUDDY, MARNIE, AND SUZI, BUT...
I CAN'T BABY-SIT FOR THEM ANYMORE.

YOU **CAN'T?** IT'S NOT BECAUSE OF WHAT HAPPENED YESTERDAY, IS IT?
UM...

WE'RE GOING TO STRAIGHTEN OUR PROBLEMS OUT, DAWN.
WE'RE GOING TO TALK TO OUR LAWYERS, AND MAYBE A COUNSELOR, TOO.

YOU WON'T HAVE ANY MORE ISSUES WITH MY EX-HUSBAND.
THAT'S NOT REALLY...

THE PROBLEM IS, UH...
I'VE HAD A LOT OF TROUBLE BECAUSE OF...

BECAUSE OF MISTAKES YOU'VE MADE.

I CAN'T BE A GOOD BABY-SITTER UNLESS THE PARENTS GIVE ME A LITTLE HELP.
I NEED TO KNOW THE IMPORTANT THINGS, LIKE ALLERGIES, AND WHERE YOU ARE WHILE I'M IN CHARGE. I NEED PHONE NUMBERS, AND ORGANIZATION.
I CAN'T DO ALL THE HOUSEWORK. AND YESTERDAY WAS VERY SCARY.
BUT MOST OF ALL...
BUDDY AND SUZI ARE STARTING TO DEPEND ON ME A LOT.
BUDDY COMES TO ME WITH SCHOOL PROBLEMS.
SUZI CALLS ME ON THE PHONE.
I LOVE BUDDY AND SUZI. AND MARNIE, TOO. BUT...
YOU'RE THEIR MOTHER... NOT ME.

I'M SORRY. THAT'S WHY I CAN'T SIT FOR YOU ANYMORE. YOUR KIDS NEED **YOU,** NOT A BABY-SITTER.
I TALKED THIS OVER WITH THE CLUB, AND THEY THINK IT'S THE RIGHT THING, TOO.

OH, DAWN. PLEASE. JUST A MINUTE.
DON'T GO.

YOU'RE THE BEST SITTER WE'VE EVER HAD. THE KIDS ADORE YOU. I DON'T KNOW WHAT THEY'D DO IF...
I'LL STILL BE IN THE NEIGHBORHOOD. WE'LL SEE EACH OTHER.

CAN'T WE WORK SOMETHING OUT?

LIKE WHAT?
WHAT IF I ASKED YOU TO COME OVER A FEW MINUTES EARLIER THAN I ACTUALLY NEED YOU?
THEN WE'D HAVE TIME TO TALK PROPERLY BEFORE I LEAVE.
AND I'LL TRY TO KEEP THE HOUSE IN BETTER SHAPE.
YOU KNOW, BUDDY AND SUZI CAN HELP YOU WITH THAT. THEY'RE GETTING GOOD AT IT.
AND MAYBE SOMETIMES I COULD LEAVE SPECIFIC CHORES FOR YOU TO DO AND PAY EXTRA.
THAT SEEMS FAIR, DOESN'T IT?
WELL...

HOW ABOUT A TRIAL?
I'LL BABY-SIT FOR YOU THREE MORE TIMES AND WE'LL SEE HOW IT GOES.
IT'S A DEAL.

SO I'LL BE SITTING FOR THEM THREE MORE TIMES.
I THINK IT WAS VERY BRAVE OF YOU TO HAVE THE TALK IN THE FIRST PLACE.
YEAH. YOU CAME TO A REASONABLE COMPROMISE.
HOW ARE THE KIDS DOING NOW, ANYWAY? SINCE THE INCIDENT?
THEY'RE GOOD, I THINK. MARNIE'S TOO LITTLE TO REMEMBER...
MALLORY TOOK GREAT CARE OF SUZI WHILE THINGS WERE GOING DOWN...

AND BUDDY'S OKAY.
HE'S CONFUSED, BUT HIS PARENTS EXPLAINED THAT THEY HAVE SOME PROBLEMS THEY'RE WORKING ON.

THE IDEA OF PARENTS KIDNAPPING THEIR OWN CHILDREN IS SCARY.
YEAH.

ring
ring
ring
ring

HELLO, BABY-SITTERS CLUB.
HI, DAWN.

HI, BUDDY.
sigh
GUESS WHAT HAPPENED IN SCHOOL TODAY?
I DROPPED MY PENCIL ON STEVE'S DESK AND MR. ZUNG SAID I COULDN'T GO TO RECESS.

BUDDY...
YEAH?
IS YOUR MOM HOME?
...YEAH.
I THINK YOU SHOULD TELL **HER** ABOUT THIS. SHE'LL HELP YOU DECIDE WHAT TO DO.
YEAH... OKAY.

WHEW.
click
WE DISCUSSED BUSINESS FOR A FEW MINUTES...
AND THEN...
ahem
I'VE BEEN THINKING ABOUT WHAT TO DO WITH THE CLUB AFTER I MOVE.
I MEAN, I KNOW WE HAVE ALL SUMMER BEFORE THAT HAPPENS, BUT I CAN'T HELP WORRYING ABOUT IT.
SO I'VE COME TO A DECISION.

MY DECISION...

IS TO RAISE OUR CLUB DUES.

WHAT?

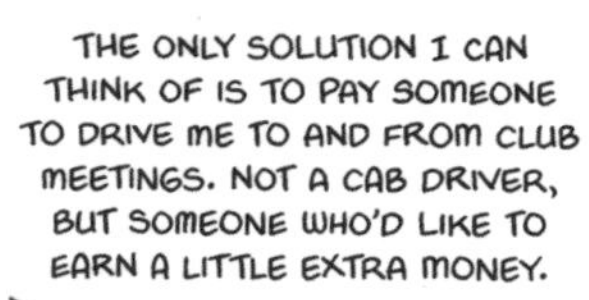
THE ONLY SOLUTION I CAN THINK OF IS TO PAY SOMEONE TO DRIVE ME TO AND FROM CLUB MEETINGS. NOT A CAB DRIVER, BUT SOMEONE WHO'D LIKE TO EARN A LITTLE EXTRA MONEY.

SOMEONE YOUNG WHO'S JUST LEARNED TO DRIVE --

CHARLIE!
CHARLIE WILL BE ABLE TO DRIVE THEN, WON'T HE?
KRISTY, THAT'S A GREAT IDEA!

AND I BET HE'LL BE **DYING** FOR EXCUSES TO USE THE CAR.

BUT...DO YOU MIND PAYING FOR IT OUT OF OUR DUES?
I KNOW IT'S KIND OF --

KRISTY, YOU'RE THE **PRESIDENT**.

IT'S THE PERFECT SOLUTION.

NO KRISTY...
NO CLUB.

HOW ABOUT NOW?
mmmm... THE RIGHT SIDE'S JUST A BIT HIGH.
NOW?
PERFECT.
DONE!
flop
WOW. IT'S LIKE A WHOLE NEW ROOM!
THIS IS SO MUCH MORE **YOU,** MARY ANNE.
I COULDN'T HAVE DONE IT WITHOUT YOU...
BOTH OF YOU.

B
S
C

ANN M. MARTIN'S The Baby-sitters Club is one of the most popular series in the history of publishing — with more than 176 million books in print worldwide — and inspired a generation of young readers. Her novels include *Belle Teal, A Corner of the Universe* (a Newbery Honor book), *Here Today, A Dog's Life,* and *On Christmas Eve,* as well as the much-loved collaborations, *P.S. Longer Letter Later* and *Snail Mail No More,* with Paula Danziger, and *The Doll People* and *The Meanest Doll in the World,* written with Laura Godwin and illustrated by Brian Selznick. She lives in upstate New York.

GALE GALLIGAN is a graduate of NYU and the Savannah College of Art and Design. Her comics have appeared in a number of anthologies, and she worked as a production assistant on *Drama* by Raina Telgemeier. Gale lives in Pleasantville, New York. Visit her online at www.galesaur.com.

DON'T MISS THE OTHER BABY-SITTERS CLUB GRAPHIC NOVELS!

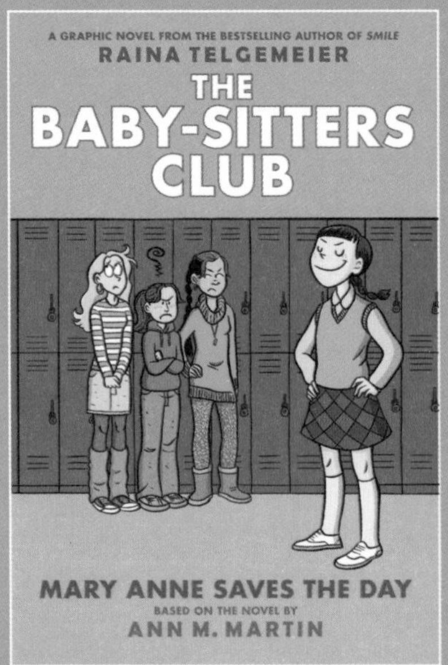